Bear & Katie

in

A Crazy Day at the Beach

Trouble in Nantucket!

Written By: Loni R. Burchett

Illustrated By: Michael Mayne

To view list of other books by Loni R. Burchett go to the last page.

A Crazy Day at the Beach—Trouble in Nantucket
First printing June 1, 2008

Copyright June 2008
U.S. Library of Congress Registration #TXU-009-609

Black Lab Publishing LLC is the owner of the Bear and Katie Series.

Written by Loni R. Burchett
Illustrated by Michael Mayne
Edited by Sherry Lynn Combs
Lay-out by Cindy Houghton

Published by Black Lab Publishing LLC
P.O. Box 64
Alton, N.H. 03809
blacklabpub@hotmail.com
www.bearandkatie.com

Printed by Morgan Press, Inc.
64 Buckley Circle
Manchester, N.H. 03103

Published and Printed in the U.S.A.

DEDICATION

Eunice Duley (aka Aunt Noonie) My wonderful Aunt who was a great influence in my life. "She was the glue that held our families together."

Andrea Gonzales (aka Tia) A great woman with a great family that I have been a part of all my life, *Te queiro y te extrano* (I love and miss you) *Tia Andrea.*

And to Bear and Katie forever: Who truly live up to the old saying; "A dog is a man's best friend."

NOTE: Bear always wears a red collar and Katie always wears a blue scarf

A SPECIAL THANKS TO THESE GREAT DOGS AND THEIR OWNERS

Max the Black Lab from Kentucky

Bronson the "Pretty White" Yellow Lab Mix from Kentucky

Casper & Wendy Poodles from Kentucky

Buster the Great Dane (Fiction)

Nike the Golden Retriever from New Hampshire

Tuckernuck the Border Collie (Fiction)

Rascal the Border Collie from Ohio

Muffy the Border Collie from Kentucky

Sea Girl the Newfoundland (Fiction)

Sybill the Rottweiler from Kentucky

Baby the Poodle from Ohio

Little Bit the Dachshund from Kentucky

Cracker the Corgie mix from Kentucky

Dozer the Schnauzer from Kentucky

Stanley (Stan) the Chow/Lab mix from Kentucky

Sugar and Honey the Yellow Labs from New Hampshire

Annie & Ruby the Golden Retrievers from Vermont

The 3 M's (Marty, Maddie & Maxwell) a Corgi, a Cocker Spaniel & a Beagle from Kentucky

Daisy May a Springer Spaniel from Virginia

Sophie the black lab/mix from New Hampshire

ACKNOWLEDGEMENTS

Nancy Grossman
Back Channel Press
Portsmouth, New Hampshire

 Sherry Lynn Combs
Adult Education Instructor
Ashland Community and Technical
College,
Ashland, Kentucky

Richard Haynes
Photographer, Professor, Artist and
Friend

Katie's Gift Shop
Rockport, MA

TABLE OF CONTENTS

INTRODUCTION

Pets play a huge role in the lives of New Englanders.

If you've ever visited New England, you have seen pets in the workplace. Almost everywhere you travel throughout the New England States, you are bound to find pets working alongside their owners. You might have a dog greet you at the door of an old country store. You might find a friendly dog follow you up and down the aisles of a gift shop as you stop to examine bottles of Maple Syrup. Or you may see a cat lying in a store window, catching a glimpse of the customers as they enter to browse.

Whether you're walking along a beach, riding in a car or sitting on a park bench, you are most likely to see someone with a pet. New Englanders *love* their pets and it's visible everywhere you look.

It's one of the things that makes life in New England so special. So if you visit a gift shop in New England, rest assure you will be greeted by a pet.

So it's no surprise that Bear and Katie love to go on trips. Their trip along the Massachusetts coast, Cape Cod and Nantucket will be a special one, when they meet up with all types of dogs. Some, just like them, are on vacation and others live and work in the stores. Bear and Katie are going to find out how special dogs *like* them really are.

So let's go now and take a trip to the beach with Bear and Katie.

Bear & Katie

in

A Crazy Day at the Beach!
Trouble in Nantucket

On the way

It's a beautiful day in New England and August is the perfect time for a trip to Cape Cod and Nantucket, which is exactly what Dad has planned for Mom and their two Black Labs, Bear and Katie. On the way to the Cape, they will travel the Massachusetts Coast, visiting many wonderful beach towns along the way. With warm temperatures this time of year the beaches will be a happy sight; especially for Bear and Katie who *love* playing in the water.

Mom is preparing a lunch for the trip and snacks for Bear and Katie. She knows Bear and Katie will want chewies and treats, so she packs them along with the lunch. "I'm sure everything is here," she thinks to herself. "Now I will call Bear and Katie."

Mom walks to the porch where Bear and Katie have been listening to Dad's stories all morning about Cape Cod and Nantucket. Katie rises to her feet with a big wiggle and then wags her tail. She walks over to nudge Bear, who has dozed off during story time. "It's time to wake up Bear," she says with a slight whine."

Bear lifts her head and lets out a huge yawn, then puts her head back down. Up it comes again accompanied by a few bigger yawns. She rises to her feet to join Katie in a big stretch. "Well-now," says Bear, with another yawn. "A little stroll through the woods and I'm ready to go!"

Dad leans back in his chair to take a drink from his cup of fresh brewed coffee. Bear and Katie nudge him with their noses, then begin licking him on the face.

"Ok, ok! I'm getting up girls; but a man sure would like to drink a good cup of coffee sometime," he tells them with a wink, wiping the Bear and Katie licks off his face. "I'm sure both of you are excited about the trip to the Cape," he adds, tipping his cup of coffee to sneak a quick gulp.

While Dad takes Bear and Katie for a walk, Mom scopes the house to make sure she hasn't forgotten anything.

"How long will it take us to get to the Cape?" ruffs Bear.

"Normally, it takes about three hours, but we won't be there until late afternoon," answers Dad. "Why so late?" questions Katie with a curious whine.

"Well, Mom wants to stop at a few stores along the way. She has a friend who just opened a new gift shop in Newburyport. She also wants to visit a few boutiques in Rockport, a small resort town near Gloucester." Dad pauses, "Glouchester is famous for its statue of "The man at the Wheel, Fisherman's Monument." We'll be sure to view the monument; then I have an appointment to look at a boat in Marblehead; that shouldn't take long," he tells them. "My plan is to spend the night in Hyannisport; take the Ferry to Nantucket first thing in the morning," he continues. "Sounds like a real exciting trip already," bark Bear and Katie.

Dad returns to the house with Bear and Katie to find Mom sitting on the porch waiting."Everything is ready to go, all we need is to pack the truck," says Mom. "We need to get our leashes?" cries Bear with a soft whine.

"Already done," answers Mom. "Well-then, let's go to the Cape!" shouts Dad. "Yeah! Let's go to the *beach*!" ruffs Bear and Katie.

The first stop is Newburyport, where Mom's friend, Kim, has a gift shop. Newburyport is a small town that sits on the Merrimack River at the mouth of the Atlantic Ocean, a town rich with federal style homes, brick sidewalks and buildings.

Dad circles the streets a few times then finally finds a place to park. "It's early, and already the gift shops are filled with tourists," says Dad.

Mom's friend Kim is happy to greet them. "It's just wonderful to see people from other places enjoying this lovely small town, I just love it here." Taking Mom by the arm, she continues. "Let me show you around."

Kim turns to Bear and Katie, "Oh, by the way! I have a helper for the store, I want you to meet," she smiles.

She leads them to her office and opens the door. "Here *Buster!* Come meet Bear and Katie," she calls.

Bear and Katie can't believe what they see. It's a huge dog; the biggest they have ever seen. "It looks like a dog, has a tail like a dog, but it's much too *big*! to be a dog," whines Bear. "It's as big as a horse!" shouts Katie with her tail tucked between her legs, backing up slowly around a corner to hide. "He's a Great Dane," says Kim. "And a big baby, I must add."

"Yes, please add," yelps Bear. "A *real* big baby, you say?"

Katie peeks her head out from the corner she's comfortably hiding behind.

"Yeah, well, too bad we don't have time to stick around and play," she grumbles.

Buster rises to his feet and walks towards Bear and Katie to greet them. Bear can't believe how huge he is, but she mustn't let Buster know that she's a little scared. Acting real *cool* she stands with her tail straight out, then looks directly at Buster. *"Hold it right there...big boy!"* she barks.

Katie, afraid Bear might anger the huge dog, nudges her. "Are you crazy!" she snarls.

Buster walks toward Bear and Katie. "Now...hang on there girls!" he winks. "I'm a

friendly Great Dane. I help Mom in the store."
Buster sits for a moment to scratch behind his ear,
then he continues. "I work here every day. It's my
job to greet customers," he barks. Bear takes a
deep breath and lets out a soft whine of relief. She
knows now that she and Katie can relax, Buster is
a friendly dog after all.

Buster is happy Bear and Katie are now relaxed
about his size. "Good dogs come in all sizes," he
snickers. So...Let me show you around the store.
We have lots of nice gifts for dogs," he ruffs! Buster
shows them the line of dog toys in Kim's shop.
Katie finds some that squeak, which is her favorite
kind of toys. She loves the squeeky sound they make.

Bear spots a yellow scarf around Buster's neck
that reads, 'Dog's Rule.' She's sure that she and
Katie need a scarf too. They begin to look around
for the scarves. Bear turns to Buster. "Hey Buster!
where did you get that scarf around your neck? I

really like it," she ruffs gently. "Well...thanks Bear, I like it too." He pauses a moment for another scratch behind his ear and then leads them to the other side of the shop where they see all sorts of scarves. "I believe this is what you're looking for, he ruffs.

Bear spots a red scarf that reads, 'Love Labs.' She's sure that's the one she wants. Katie finds a blue scarf that reads, "Hug a Lab!." Bear and Katie pick up the scarves with their teeth and take them to Dad.

Dad chuckles and gladly puts them on his two precious dogs. "Now don't you two look great!" he says with a big smile and a proud voice. Mom pays for the scarves and says good-bye to her friend, but she promises to visit again soon and, of course, bring Bear and Katie to spend time with Buster.

A short time later they arrived in Rockport on Cape Ann. The beautiful rocky coast is lined with lovely homes, and lobster boats fill the harbor. With just one look you can see why it's called *Rockport.* While Mom browses the art galleries and boutiques to find what she is looking for, Dad walks Bear and Katie around the gorgeous town and out on several piers.

Suddenly Katie spots a gift shop that bears her name. "Look!...It says Katie's," she barks. She's so excited, she quickly runs into the store. "Hurry, Bear, hurry! Look, they have scarves here too, and these scarves have names!" She barks even louder.

Dad and Bear follow Katie into the store. "I'll look for a red scarf that says Bear!" she ruffs. "And...oh look! Here's a blue one that says Katie!" she exclaims. Bear and Katie reach for the scarves with their teeth and turn to Dad. Dad gently reaches for them and nods. Bear and Katie watch Dad approach the checkout counter with matching smiles. "I think I will buy these for my dogs," he says, handing the scarves to the lady at the counter with a wink. "And...I guess we can throw in this Frisbee too," he chuckles."

Dad turns to Bear and Katie with a happy grin."Now, you two will have to wait until we get home before you can wear the scarves. So, no more scarf hunting, ok? However, we do have this new Frisbee to play with when we get to the beach." Bear and Katie share a few barks.

Bear and Katie don't care to wait to wear the scarves because they are already wearing the ones Mom bought earlier at Kim's shop in Newbury-port. "I like this shop. It has a lot of nice things for dogs," says Bear with a long happy wail. "I like this shop because it has my name," says Katie with a big yelp! Everyone in Katie's gift shop turns to look at the two labs and laughs.

The family leaves Rockport and heads straight to Gloucester only a few miles away. The town is well known for its huge fishing industry and the famous statue of a fisherman looking out at sea, with his hand on the helm in a storm. Dad and Mom are anxious to see the statue called, "Man at the Wheel." Bear and Katie get their picture taken in front of the statue. Before they leave, Dad and Mom take a moment to read the plaque that bears the names of the hundreds of brave fishermen who lost their lives at sea.

They turn to walk toward the truck with Bear and Katie. Dad is happy to be on his way to Mar-

blehead, a lovely resort town just North of Boston." On a beautiful clear day like today you can see the skyline of Boston in the distance," Dad tells everyone. Dad's not shy about his love for Boston, the place he calls "Bean Town." He's proud to let everyone know he's a true fan of the Celtics, Patriots, Bruins, and of course Bear and Katie's favorite team in all the world, the *Red Sox!*

Bear and Katie are enjoying their trip to the Cape and all the places they visit on the way there. Just a turn off the main road and they enter the narrow streets of Marblehead.

"This small town, called Marblehead, was once a thriving fishing industry. In fact, it was once the fishing capitol of the world. Cod fish, I believe it was," says Mom. "Today it's called the 'yacht capital of the world,' because of yacht races held each year, and of course sailboat races are also held here each year," explains Mom.

"Something is always happening here in Marble-head," she adds.

Dad stops at the marina to talk with a man about a boat he seems to like. After a short time he returns . He removes Bear and Katie's leashes and help them into the truck. "I've decided to keep looking around. I'm looking for something a little bigger," he continues.

"We still have time plenty of time, so, let's make a stop in Boston before we continue to the Cape. Maybe pick up some nice souveniers."

Only eighteen miles down the road, they arrive in Boston. The first place they visit is what Bosto-nians call the 'North End.' There, Dad and Mom take Bear and Katie to see the home of Paul Re-vere; famous for his ride through Boston during the Revolutionary War, In the early days of America. Bear and Katie are amazed when they see the statue of the man on his horse. "This is Paul Revere," says Mom. " He rode his horse through the streets of Boston shouting, "The British are coming!"

"I guess in those days they didn't have a good dog," chuckles Katie, followed by a few barks from Bear.

Before leaving the 'North End,' Mom stops at the famous out-door Italian Market where the freshest veggies and fruit in Boston can be found. She picks out a few apples to snack on.

Next, they visit the Boston Commons. A huge park in the center of town where everyone includ- ing Bear and Katie take a ride on one of the parks Swan Boats, in the parks pond. Then it's a tour of Cheers, named for a popular T.V. show. Then it's off to the Boston Aquarium. Bear and Katie are really enjoying themselves so much, that Dad decides to show them Harvard University. "This is the greatest College in the U.S.!" Boast Dad. "It's famous for it's medical school not to mention, it has the best law school in the world."

After a trip through Harvard, Dad and Mom take Bear and Katie for a stroll in a park along the Charles River. Just across the Arthur Fielder Bridge, they find a nice spot to sit. "This will be a nice place to eat lunch," says Mom. "We can look at the hatch shell, home of the Boston Pops, and pretend we are listening to the wonderful orchestra play."

Mom takes out the lunch she packed and they all enjoy a quiet time to eat and watch the sail-boats move slowly up and down the Charles River.

After a nice rest, they continue their tour. It's off to Quincy Market and a trip aboard 'Old Ironsides.' A ship used during the Revolutionary War. But a trip through Boston isn't complete until they see

Fenway Park, home of the Boston Red Sox. Bear and Katie's favorite baseball team. "I'm sure Dad will be buying tickets and trying to sneak both of you into a game," says Mom, while nodding her head at Dad. A picture of Bear and Katie in front of the 'Green Monster' completes their tour of Boston. They return to the truck. "now it's time to head on down to the Cape!" Says Dad anxiously.

Bear lies her head down to rest. Katie peers out the window and watches Boston fade from site.

They arrive in Hyannisport later in the afternoon. Mom is pleased that the hotel is across from the dock where they will be taking the ferry to Nantucket Island. "I think we should eat first," says Mom, then she pauses. "I want to do one more thing before we call it a day."

"What would that be?" questions Dad, looking a bit puzzled. "I want to go to the library before it closes to see the exhibit of the Kennedy family," she answers. Dad quickly replies, "Oh, of course! We all should see the exhibit, after all, John F. Kennedy was one of our greatest Presidents," he says, looking at Bear and Katie.

After dinner, they walk through the lovely town of Hyannisport until they arrive at the library just before dusk. Walking up the sidewalk toward the entrance, they see a man inside approaching the door with keys in his hand. He opens the door slightly and calls to them. "I was just getting ready to close for the night; you are my last visitors," he yells with a friendly voice.

He motions for them to enter and points to the other side of the library. "Over here we have a wonderful exhibit of Senator Ted Kennedy, John F. Kennedy, Robert Kennedy, and on the other side; there's a gigantic photo of the entire Kennedy family and a special memorial of John. He pauses a moment as if to remember him. "John Kennedy Jr.," he smiles. "Enjoy yourselves, and if you have any questions, feel free to ask," he says with pride as he walks away.

Mom and Dad take time to read everything. They browse around the small library looking at every picture with great admiration. The wonderful tour puts Dad in a proud mood and happy to be an American.

As they leave the library and walk back to the hotel, everyone is exhausted and ready for bed. Tomorrow they will be catching the early ferry to the Island. Mom wants to arrive in Nantucket early enough to find a great spot on the beach and she knows that the boat ride is almost two hours long.

Katie jumps on a bed across the room and wiggles her way into a comfortable position, while Bear slowly walks around and looks at the top of the bed where she sees a pillow just waiting for her. She leaps on the bed and buries her head in the pillow. The two labs quickly fall asleep.

Aboard the Ferry

It's early when Mom wakes everyone. She's anxious for Dad to feed and walk Bear and Katie so they can go to the boat dock in time to catch the first ferry leaving for Nantucket.

Before they board, Bear stops for a flash-back moment, remembering Katie falling off the ferry going to Islesboro, Maine, searching for a treasure.

"You better be careful, Katie," orders Bear. "This ferry is taking us much farther out to sea than the one in *Islesboro.*"

"I promise you, I won't be doing any swimming until we get to the beach. You won't catch me falling off of *this* boat," answers Katie with a growl, a little annoyed at Bear's comment.

Suddenly, Bear's attention is focused on the other side of the boat, where she spots a gorgeous Golden Retriever looking at her. Bear nudges Katie to get her attention. "Look Katie, it's a Golden Retriever. He must be going to Nantucket too. "Wow! He sure is handsome," ruffs Katie. "You can say that again," barks Bear. "Wow! He sure is handsome," ruffs Katie again. "Ok-wise guy. Oops! I mean wise girl," chuckles Bear with a short whine.

Bear and Katie are having fun teasing each other. They're happy to see another dog aboard the boat. "Let's walk over and introduce ourselves," suggest Bear.

The two of them walk to the other side of the boat to get a closer look at who they hope will be their new friend. ."Hello, my name is Bear and this is my best friend Katie."

"A girl named Bear?" questions the pretty golden dog. "What's wrong with a girl name Bear?"

grumbles Bear. "I looked like a little bear cub when I was a puppy and my owners named me *Bear*. I like my name quite well; Thank you." answers Bear with her nose in the air and wagging her tail.

"Sorry Bear, I didn't mean to offend you. My name is Nike. I'm a Golden Retriever, and I'm from Lake Sunapee" he tells them with a whine and a big yawn that sounds like a screech. "You mean like the shoe?" questions Katie, nudging her way in front of Bear.

Embarrassed by Katie's question, Bear pokes Katie with her nose. Katie ruffs a few snickers to Bear. "I was just getting even for you," she ruffs, then quickly changes the subject. "Do you know Ruby and Annie, two Golden Retrievers who live in Vermont?" woofs Katie, now standing nose to nose with Bear. "They work at a country store in Taftsville," says Bear pushing her way back in front of Katie.

"When we visit them we have lots of fun. Annie follows us around the store and Ruby greats everyone at the door." continues Bear. "Then we go in their back yard to play ball and visit while Mom

shops around for her favorite maple products."
She pauses. "Have you ever been there?" she questions.

Nike takes a moment to think. With his paw he rubs his eye and then his chin. "No, I don't believe I know those two dogs or have ever been to Vermont, Bear, but I sure will keep it in mind. Golden Retrievers, mmm...."

"Well...those two dogs work every day," ruffs Katie.

"Since you mention working, I'm on my way to help my Aunt Pauline. She has a gift shop in Nantucket," Nike tells them.

Looking at each other they both have the same thing in mind. They will be sure to visit Aunt Pauline's store to visit their new friend Nike.

Suddenly Dad approaches them. "Hey! What's going on girls?" he says, petting them on the head.

Dad thinks he has caught Bear and Katie flirting. "Handsome dog, isn't he?" comments Dad. "Ok...if you like Golden Retrievers," ruffs Bear, shying away. "yeah...if you like Golden Retrievers," yelps Katie as they turn and walk away..

A short time later the ferry makes its way through the harbor at Nantucket Sound, passing the lighthouse and the long elbow of sand dunes. As the boat slowly enters the harbor, Bear and Katie can see the beautiful pier boasting of giftshops boutiques and art galleries. As they near the dock, the magnificent smell of flowers fills the air. Dad and Mom can see why the charming town with its lovely gray homes and buildings earned its name, "little gray lady of the sea."

Everyone is anxious to exit the ferry and browse the shops along the pier. Mom loves the wonderful aroma of flowers. She tilts her head for a moment and takes a deep breath to catch the fragrance.

"What a fabulous place! It's so beautiful and it smells so fresh. I could stay here forever," she says.

Looking down at a brochure in her hand she begins to read, "This Island was settled in 1659. The Wampanoag Indian Tribe called it "Far away Land." Bear and Katie listen anxiously about the history of the Nantucket while Dad turns his eyes to the boats. "I believe I'll have time to look at some boats while we are here," he mumbles to himself.

"Wow! Check out Main Street," ruffs Bear. "The rocky street leads all the way down here to the water!"

Katie is curious about the rocky street. "Why is the street made of rocks?" cries Katie.

"First of all, the street was made from rocks, or should I say, *cobblestones,*" explains Dad. "The *cobblestones* actually came from the ship's ballast, and were used to build the street over two hundred years ago, during the "Whaling Era." It was much too hard to slide the huge fish through the sand, so the fisherman built the *cobblestone* streets. When the cobblestones are wet, they are slippery, which made it easy to pull the huge fish ashore, so that is why Main Street is very long, and the *cobblestones* stretch all the way down to the water." He continues, "Nantucket was once a famous whaling port. We'll learn more about it when we visit the Whaling Museum."

Mom is fascinated by the beautiful rose covered cottages made of cedar siding. Flowers are everywhere, they cover the roof tops while the sidewalks are lined with tulips. Even the fences are draped with roses.

Mom is happy when she spots the cute cottage Dad reserved, It's just like the houses along main street-a gorgeous Cape Cod with flower pots built under the windows seals, with a huge trestle of flowers draped over the roof. "This is absolutely beautiful!," she says with a gasp.

"Let's not waste one moment, and get to the beach," ruffs Katie. "Yeah! I want to look for some sea shells," barks Bear. "How about we get inside and unpack, change into our swim suits and head to the beach?" shouts Dad.

At the Beach

"Well, now! Let's go to the beach," says Mom with a pleasant smile. Dad reaches for a blanket and towels. Mom reaches for her camera and treats for Bear and Katie.

The Beach is just a short walk from the cottage. Bear and Katie pick up the pace when they spot the sand and the lifeguard sitting in his chair. Bear and Katie pass a lot of people lying on blankets soaking in the sun. Children are making sand castles, burying themselves with sand, and tossing beach balls to each other.

Mom finds a perfect spot to spread-out their blanket. She places an umbrella in the sand for a shade. Dad opens the beach chairs, and they both sit for a moment to remove their shoes for a walk along the water.

"Let's walk along the rocks to look for sea shells first and then dip our feet in the water when the waves come in," barks Bear. "Great idea!" replies Katie with a soft whine.

Dad and Mom walk slowly along the edge of the water enjoying the waves as they roll over their feet. Dad tells Bear and Katie to stay at an eye's view of them, as they rush to the rocks to look for sea shells.

Bear begins to look for sea shells in one direction and Katie in another. Katie suddenly spots a crab between two rocks and begins to sniff it. She jumps from one rock to another turning around and around, and sniffing again and again. She begins to bark to get Bear's attention.

Turning, Bear meets up with Katie to see what she has found. "Look, Bear, it's a crab!" cries Katie with a sharp whine. "There are crabs everywhere.!"

"Look over here! ruffs Bear. "I found an old lobster trap. It must have washed up on shore during high tide. This looks like a good place to look for sea shells," she continues, all excited.

Katie begins to help Bear look for sea shells, but after a short time she realizes she doesn't want to spend all day at the beach looking for sea shells. "Bear," she barks. "Let's find something more entertaining."

"This is entertaining enough for me," answers Bear, sniffing for shells. "Oh, you go ahead and sniff for shells, Bear, This is fun, but I want to do something *real exciting*," barks Katie.

"*Real* exciting! *Well*, I'm perfectly content looking for sea shells and walking along the beach as the waves splash at my paws. And I love the sound of the waves; it's so...soothing to my ears," exclaims Bear.

"Ok then, go splash your paws in the water. I think I will just wonder a bit farther along the rocks." whines Katie.

Well...then if you don't want to look for sea shells, I'll head back where Dad and Mom are on the beach. I'll let them know you are wondering around at the rocks a while longer. Maybe I'll take a nap," says Bear, with a disappointed yawn.

"And don't be getting into trouble," she continues.

"What kind of trouble can I get into just walking on the beach?" snarls Katie.

"What kind of trouble? *Huh!*" mumbles Bear as she walks away. "Katie always finds trouble! That dog's name should be *trouble*."

Bear returns to where Dad and Mom have placed their blanket. Dad spots Bear and waves to her. Bear lies down under the umbrella and watches Mom and Dad as they stroll along the water's edge. She closes her eyes and slightly drifts off to a light sleep.

Meanwhile, Katie wanders a short distance from the rocks and hears a crowd of people shouting. Curiously, she walks towards the crowd where she spots a group gathered by a large net stretched across the sand. Katie's eyes become fixed on a volleyball.

"Oh Wow! Just what I'm looking for a good game of *retrieve the ball!* She picks up her pace as she gets closer to the volleyball net. Katie isn't paying attention to where she is walking until people begin to shout at her. Katie is stepping on blankets, towels, clothes and with her paws she is tossing sand everywhere along the way. But for Katie, only one thing is on her mind-the *ball.* "If I'm lucky, I'll be playing ball soon. Oh boy! I can't wait! Everyone knows Labs are friendly, playful, and excellent retrievers," she thinks to herself.

Katie is so excited that she pays no attention to a woman who is sun-bathing, and she tosses sand on the woman's face with her paws as she passes by. The woman is so angry as she wipes the sand off of her face and sun glasses. "Oh...! I *hate* dogs!" she frets.

Katie finally reaches the volleyball players. She barks a friendly greeting and sits in the begging position. She knows that if she puts on the sad face someone will notice her, *and* it works!

A muscular man with a shaved head approaches Katie. "Hey girl, where did you come from?" he asks, rubbing Katie on the head.

"I'm Vinnie, and you are...? asks the man.
"Katie...I'm Katie."

"Well Katie, I bet you would like to play some ball? All Labs like to play ball, *don't they?*"

Katie quickly answers him with a loud bark and wag of her tail.

The man holds up a yellow volleyball and chuckles. "Okay, girl, *you're in*!"

Katie loves it, running after the ball each time it goes too far from the net and pushing it back with her nose. All the players are cheering Katie. Katie's having so much fun she begins to show off; running with the ball and jumping in the air, running around the net and even rolling in the sand. Katie is *one* happy dog, but she is completely unaware she is annoying the woman who is trying to get a tan. Each time Katie shakes herself off, she flings sand on everyone around her including the woman who hates dogs.

Katie continues to anger the woman who is now sitting comfortably, enjoying the ocean air. The soft breeze and sunshine make it a perfect day to get a tan. The woman picks up a bottle of suntan lotion; pours a small amount in her hand. Just as she begins to apply it to her arm, Katie nearly falls on top of the woman, when she catches her right paw on the lining of the woman's blanket. Katie begins to twist and turns to free her paw, slapping the woman on the face with her tail and knocking the bottle of suntan lotion from the woman's hand. The lotion runs from the bottle and all over the woman, down the blanket and onto her sunglasses. The woman is covered with sand and lotion from head to toe. It's such a funny sight everyone begins to laugh.

But the woman, who is now covered with sand from head to toe, doesn't think it's funny and is boiling mad at Katie. She searches through her beach bag looking for her cell phone. "I'll fix that dog!" she frets.

Katie gets Arrested!

With a towel, the woman wipes sand from her face and hands so she can dial 911. "When I'm finished with that dog, it won't be playing volleyball for a very, very-long time," she continues.

The woman successfully reaches an officer. "There's a *dangerous* dog on the beach growling and chasing children. I'm afraid it will bite one of them. You must hurry!" she tells the officer. "We'll be right there!" answers the anxious officer.

Katie nor the volleyball players are aware that the police have been called, or that Katie is in trouble, so they continue to play.

Bear wakes from a short snooze and realizes Katie is out of sight and has been gone too long. She begins to worry and quickly goes to Dad to tell him that Katie is missing. Bear has a feeling something has happened to her. Dad looks at his watch and notices it's been more than ten minutes since he last saw Katie walking along the rocks. "A dog can go a long ways in ten minutes," he mumbles. "I lost track of time enjoying the waves and ocean views. We need to find Katie right away!"

Bear begins to look around and bark, but Katie doesn't hear her. Dad and Mom follow Bear to the other end of the beach where they find two kids kicking a beach ball. Bear knows that she and Katie love to play with kids, especially the game they call, retrieve the ball.

"Have you seen a black dog with a blue scarf around her neck that says, 'Hug a Lab?' asks Dad.

"No sir!" replies a boy holding the beach ball. "But I sure hope you find your dog!" he shouts.

Bear has gone in the wrong direction on the beach but, is still sniffing frantically to pick up Katie's trail.

But on the opposite side of the beach a patrol truck drives into the parking lot and stops. A handsome dog, a Border Collie, standing nearby, hides behind a car, thinking the patrol office is after him. He quickly realizes the officer is looking for the Black Lab chasing a volleyball.

The handsome dog is about to become Katie's friend.

The officer reaches for a leash and begins to walk toward Katie. The officer is surprised he doesn't see any children running from a dangerous dog or a dog growling at anyone. He only sees

Katie standing near the volleyball players having fun, but he continues his job.

"Stand back everyone! I'm here to pick up this dangerous dog!" he says. "Dangerous dog! What dangerous dog?" shouts Vinnie, the muscular man with the shaved head. "I got a call about a dangerous dog and I am taking this black Lab to the dog patrol station.!" shouts the officer. "*I'm just doing my job!* "he continues.

Katie begins to look around for her best friend Bear, who is looking for her at the other end of the beach. She begins to whine as the officer reaches under Katie's scarf to find her collar. "I'm innocent," she cries. "I...I'm just a fun-loving, friendly dog playing a game of *retrieve the ball. Please... don't take me!*" cries Katie.

The officer ignores Katie's plea and begins to pull her toward his truck. Katie puts up a struggle and then gives in. She doesn't want to make matters worse. The crowd pleads with the officer, but he continues to tug on Katie until she is in his truck. The angry crowd turns to look at the woman whom they believe called the police on Katie.

The woman happily watches the officer take Katie away, then turns to the crowd with a smug look, tilts her head in the air, and mumbles a few words to herself as she turns to look away from the crowd.

The Border Collie, who was hiding, steps out from behind the car and walks towards the crowd. "Attention everyone!" barks the dog. "I'm 'Tuckernuck, but everyone calls me Tucker.

I'm Nantucket's famous Border Collie, And I'm here to tell you Katie will be fine. Just leave everything to me!" barks the handsome dog.

Tucker quickly turns and heads toward the beach to notify Katie's family and catches up with Bear, barking as he runs.

Bear stops to see the dog making all the commotion.

"I believe you are looking for Katie!" barks Tucker anxiously. "Why, yes!" whines Bear loudly. "Do you know where she is?"

"She was picked up by the Dog Patrol, just a few minutes ago!" barks Tucker.

Bear becomes frightened, and quickly barks to get Dad and Mom's attention.

Dad and Mom hear Bear's bark and know that it's her bark of danger. They rush to meet up with

Bear. "What is it Bear?" ask Dad. "It's Katie. She's been picked up by the Dog Patrol," whines Bear.

Dad reaches out to rub Bear on the head, "Don't worry Bear. We'll just go pick her up."

"It's not going to be that easy," ruffs Tucker. "You see, the woman lied. She said Katie was chasing children and trying to bite them. You know what, they do to dogs that bite or are dangerous? They don't let them go. They....well...we have to do something fast! Very fast!" he continues with a sharp bark.

"What can we do?" cries Bear, worried about her best friend Katie. "First of all, we have to be strong, and smart!" ruffs Tucker.

"I'm smart!" snickers Bear.

"Dad and Mom's job will be to stay at the beach to gather witnesses from the volleyball game. Bear, you and I will gather, what I call *the dogs of Nantucket,* woofs Tucker. "That woman who fibbed about Katie doesn't know who she is messing with until she meets the *dogs of Nantucket,*" he barks.

"By the way, I'm Tuckernuck, Nantucket's famous Border Collie, but you can call me Tucker," woofs the proud black and white dog.

Tucker and Bear begin visiting the shops in town. Tucker takes one side of the street and Bear takes the other that leads to the pier.

Tucker stops at a shop on the end of town. "Sophie! Are you there?" he barks.

Sophie walks out from behind a counter.

"What's up Tucker?" she woofs.

"We have a dog accused of chasing and frightening children. But it's not true. I was there. The dog was playing volleyball," he ruffs.

"The dog was arrested for playing volleyball? Dogs play volleyball all the time on Nantucket beaches," ruffs Sophie.

"Well...it was a little more than that. She got a little carried away and began to run too close to a woman, knocking a bottle of suntan lotion out of her hand," answers Tucker, pausing, for a slight chuckle. "It's a Black Lab name, Katie," he adds. "She's at the dog station where they took my sister Rascal."

"Rascal was picked up too? Oh my! What has Rascal done now?" she asks.

"She was visiting her friends who live at the Cranberry Farm and was accused of stealing cranberries. Of course, we all know it couldn't be true because the cranberries aren't ripe yet," answers Tucker. "Rascal only likes cranberries when they are bright red. I think the woman who accused Rascal is the same woman who called the Dog Patrol on Katie.

Sophie jumps in the air and spins around. "A black Lab you say? I'm a black Lab! We swim and chase balls," she sighs. "We *must* help Katie right away-and, of course, Rascal too. "

"Here is the plan," ruffs Tucker, whispering in Sophie's ear.

"Got it!" answers Sophie. I have a friend named Daisy-Mae, she's a Springer Spaniel with a really cute speckeled snout, her owners have a great paper shop down the street. I'll go there to get a banner made. Then I'll meet you at the station where they hold all the dogs," she ruffs as she runs out of the gift shop and across the street.

Tucker has one more stop, a visit with some friends he calls 'The Three M's': Maxwell, Marty and Maddie. Maxwell, a Beagle mix, has a keen nose for sniffing out clues and Marty, the Welsh Corgie, is slow in walk but very distinguished and always ready to use his charm to gather a crowd. While Maddie, the Cocker Spaniel, is known as one of the best guard dogs in Nantucket.

"I need your help," barks Tucker, greeting his friends with a high five.

"Say no more!" replies Marty the distinguished Corgie. "We've already heard that Rascal and a Lab were arrested. *Oops*...I mean picked up by the Dog Patrol. From what I understand, there's a woman who is accusing dogs of crimes they didn't commit. My friend Dozer, a fine Schnauzer, and a sweet poodle friend of mine name Baby, was also arrested. *Darn...I mean picked up*," he adds, shaking his head. "If we don't do something about that woman, we'll all be...*picked up*, so...just tell us what you want us to do!"

Tucker is pleased to know Maxwell, Marty and Maddie, 'The Three M's' are ready to work. He gives them instructions and is off to the next store.

Marty tells Maxwell the Beagle to gather all the locals he can and to meet him at the Whaling Museum. He wants to be sure to tell everyone their precious pooches are in danger. He sends Maddie the Cocker Spaniel to the patrol station to guard and to keep watch until Sophie gets there.

Bear is at the other end of town near the boat dock telling her story to dogs and their owners everywhere she goes. They all want to help Katie.

"I have a fine Rottweiler," says one man. "Her name is Sybill. She's such a sweet and gentle dog. And...trust me...she's *always* misunderstood," says the man. "She would love to help."

Another man, who is getting his lobster boat ready for a trip out to sea, hears Bear's desperate barks for help.

"I couldn't help but overhear what you said about your friend Katie. I have a wonderful Newfoundland who works on my boat with me, and, like Labs, she *loves* the water. She also has a great reputation here on the island for helping children learn to swim. Her name is Sea Girl, because she loves the sea, of course. I will bring her along to help Katie," he tells Bear.

As Bear walks away, the man waves his hand to get Bear's attention. "I also have a friend in Chatham, over on the Cape, who owns a handsome Lab/Chow mix, named Stanley, but he calls him Stan. Now *that* dog is a quick thinker!" says the man, shaking his finger. "I'll give my friend a call." Bear is happy that she has found so many who want to help Katie. Now it's time to return to the

beach to see what Tucker has in mind next, and
to see how Dad and Mom have done rounding
up witnesses.

On the way to the beach, Bear spots a *noisy*
group of dogs and quickly joins them. "These are
my friends," barks Tucker. "Let me introduce
them."

Bear is happy to see so many dogs join in to
help. "My black Lab friend Max is from Martha's
Vineyard; we go back a long ways," ruffs Tucker.
"This is Muffy, our Border Collie friend who works
at the cranberry farm Rascal and I *love* to visit," he
adds. "And my two Poodle friends are, Wendy and
Casper; my Boxer friend Shaybee, and that handsome white dog is Bronson, and we mustn't forget
these two yellow Lab sisters, Sugar and Honey," he
tells Bear with a satisfying bark.

Bear looks at all the different dogs with a cheer-ful smile, and in the crowd is Nike the golden re-triever she and Katie met on the boat ride to the island.

"Now, here's the plan," barks Tucker all excited.

"Shaybee the Boxer and Bronson the handsome white dog will run and catch up with Sophie. My friend Marty is gathering a crowd to meet us at the Whaling Museum. Then we will all meet Sophie at the dog station," says Tucker, with a happy bark.

Bear is happy about the work Tucker has done for her best friend Katie. Now it's off to see what Dad and Mom have accomplished.

Meanwhile Katie is taken to a place out of town. As she is removed from the patrolman's truck, she can hear dogs barking. The barks are not happy barks. They're barks of frightened dogs, and Katie is frightened too. The patrolman takes her into a large building and forces her into a cage, only to lock it.

"I'm innocent!" she cries.

"I'm sorry, ol' girl...but, I'm just doing my job."
He exclaims. "If I felt sorry for every dog that comes
in here and let them go free, I wouldn't have a job."

A Border Collie lying on the floor lifts her head
and ruffs.

"Forget it. He's not going to help you. It's going
to take a dog to help us. I know as soon as my
brother Tucker finds out I'm in here he will be
working on my release, and If any dog can do it,

it's him! He's the famous Nantucket Border Collie. And I'll bet he'll be working on getting you out of here, too," grumbles the pretty black and white dog.

"My name is Katie, and I was just playing volley-ball when a woman on the beach called the dog catcher, or should I say, the Dog Patrol Officer. That's what they like to be called these day," she wines. "My name is Rascal, and I'm told, I live up to my name. Seems like I'm always in a fix," Rascal barks.

"Seems like I'm always in a fix too," ruffs Katie shaking her head.

"Why are you here?" asks Katie with a short whine. "Well, I was visiting my friend Muffy, ear-lier, who works at a Cranberry farm, and a tourist told the owner she saw me stealing cranberries. It wasn't true at all," she cries.

Katie gets a curious look on her face and rubs a paw across her chin. "I wonder if we've been accused by the same woman?" Rascal takes her paw and rubs her chin too. "I...wonder!"

Katie and Rascal have a feeling it's the same woman and that woman doesn't like dogs.

"If Tucker can find our friends Muffy and the two poodles Casper and Wendy, they will surely help," sighs Rascal, with her head lying down resting on her paws.

"Do you live on Nantucket?" asks Katie.

"My brother Tucker and I came here last year from the Vineyard, Martha's Vineyard, that is," answers the shy Border Collie. "I'm a famous Frisbee player. People come from everywhere to watch me play," she adds. "My brother is famous around Nantucket because he was named after the legend of the Tuckernuck ghost, on Tuckernuck Island." Rascal pauses a moment. "Haven't you heard of the *Tuckernuck Ghost?*"

"Sorry, friend, but I never heard of Tuckernuck Island or any ghost." answers Katie. "Well then, you'll have to come back sometime around Halloween and we'll take you to Tuckernuck and you'll learn all about the Tuckernuck ghost. *It's real!*" ruffs Rascal.

"I have a Frisbee tournament on Martha's Vineyard next week, so I know Tucker will be working real hard to get me released." he continues.

Wow! a Frisbee champion, you say?" Well, my owner bought us a Frisbee to play with on the beach. If we get out of here, we'll get together for a game."

"I'm sure Tucker is working on a plan to get us out of here," replies Rascal.

"I'll bet you're right! And Bear is probably working on it too," sighs Katie

"Don't forget about me," cries a small white poodle sitting in the cage next to Katie. "They call me Baby."

Rascal looks at the small poodle, "We won't forget you, Baby."

Bear, Tucker, and all the dogs around Nantucket have caught up with Dad and Mom at the beach. "Did you get the information from the volleyball players?" cries Bear anxiously. "Yes!" says Mom. "And not only did we get the information from the players, but they are going to meet us in front of the Whaling Museum. It's quite a walk from here so we better get a move on," she says.

The *dogs of Nantucket* walk towards the museum barking all the way. As they get closer to the museum, they pass by the boat dock where the last ferry to Hyannisport is about to leave the island. Tucker spots the woman who accused Katie of chasing children in the group of passengers. Tucker tells Bear as they walk past slowly, keeping their eyes fixed on the woman.

Dad notices the volleyball players in front of the museum as well as the many locals who have rallied around Marty, the distinguished Corgie. "Finally, we are all together!" shouts Vinnie.

Out of nowhere two small dogs appear."Wait for us!" they bark. Tucker just laughs, "Well, come on Little Bit and Cracker." He continues, "These are two of Nantucket's sweetest dogs." The reddish brown Dachshund is LIttle Bit and the little light brown dog is a mix of ? Her name is Cracker and

she's an angel." All the dogs bark in agreement.

"Now we can continue," barks Tucker.

Vinnie, the volleyball player steps forward.
"First of all, we need to find the woman, take her

to the Patrol Officer, and make her tell the truth,"
he says with a loud voice. All the dogs begin to
bark. Bear's bark can be heard over top of all the
dogs. "I just saw the woman," they hear her say.
"She's getting ready to board the ferry, and it's the
last one to leave for the night."

Tucker jumps in. "We have to stop that boat!"
ruffs Tucker.

"We mustn't waste a moment," shouts Vinnie,
waving his hand to motion everyone to quickly follow him.

The Volleyball players, the locals and the dogs
run down the street and onto Main Street and to
the ferry.

"Hold it right there!" shouts Vinnie. "Don't move
that boat!" yell the locals of Nantucket. "We are a
community who love animals," cries the man with

Sea Dog, the huge Newfoundland, by his side. "Hold that boat!" shouts the man with Sybil, the Rottie.

Bear spots the woman boarding the boat. "Stop that woman!" she barks, snarls and growls. The other dogs join in with barks, snarls and growls.

The woman tries to take her baggage and run, but she is stopped by two golden retrievers. "Why, it's Annie and Ruby!" ruffs Bear. "It's my friends from Vermont! All right!" Bear smiles, wagging her tail.

Everyone gathers around the woman, while Wendy and Casper, the two poodles, grab at her luggage. All the dogs begin to bark.

"Ok...ok!" yells the frightened woman, "What do you want?"

"We want you to tell the truth about Katie," yells Vinnie "And the truth about Rascal," adds Tucker.

"Alright, alright, I'll go tell the patrol officer that Katie didn't chase the children. Just get these *mutts* away from me," she yells.

Tucker steps forward with a long growl. The woman continues, "And...I'll tell them that Rascal didn't steal any cranberries," she tells the crowd.

Everyone cheers and quickly begins to head towards the patrol station, when suddenly a bus driver spots the crowd to offer them a ride.

"Where is everyone going, in such a hurry?" asks the driver. "To the dog jail to pick up the dogs who were picked up because this woman told fibs," answers Vinnie, smiling and rubbing his shaved head.

"Well, climb aboard!" says the driver. "I was on my way to park the bus when I saw this crowd, but I happen to love animals, too. I have a cat you know. His name is Jasper, and I wouldn't want anyone to fib about him," he continues, giving the woman a long stare. Bear and Tucker make her sit in the front roll seat.

When they arrive, Sophie is already there with Shaybee and Bronson and other dogs, and even some cats they picked up on the way. They have a banner stretched across the entrance of the Dog Station.

It reads, "Free Katie, Rascal, Dozer and Baby!."

The woman is nervous when she tells the officer she lied about Katie and Rascal, then she goes on to tell that all the other dogs were there because of her. The officer is so angry he lets all the dogs go home with their owners. "I'm letting them go," he shouts, " but they must be on a leash, except for the beaches that don't require them, or they will end up back here again," he orders.

After telling the truth, the woman is ordered to stay on the Island for one week and take care of the dogs who were brought into the dog station. She will feed, water and clean up after them. She quickly realizes she won't be telling any *fibs* about dogs anymore.

Katie and Rascal have had plenty of time to become friends and to discuss their reckless behavior. They both vow to try (try, that is!)to be better at obeying orders. They learned an important lesson: to stay close to loved ones when at large gatherings.

Dozer the Schnauzer and Baby the Poodle run to their owners and jump in their arms. Rascal runs to her brother Tucker, jumping over him and back again. Tucker just laughs. "That's my Rascal!," he ruffs happily.

Dad, Mom and Bear are relieved to see Katie. They know that Katie would never try to chase a child. But they hope Katie realizes how close they came to losing her.

Bear decides to show how happy she is by jumping in the air, followed by a few spins.

Katie is so happy to see everyone, she begins running in circles and already barking about going sightseeing. "I sure would like to visit the famous Whaling Museum," ruffs Katie, "and maybe a bite to eat on the way to visit the Cranberry Farm tomorrow.

I also want to be in the crowd watching Rascal play Frisbee on Martha's Vineyard."

Bear just laughs at her friend Katie. "Next week we are going to Martha's Vineyard. We will visit the Gayhead Light and the famous 'Black Dog' restaurant. Do you think you can keep out of trouble there?"

"Are you kidding, Bear! I'm not going to leave your sight," she snickers. "Did you say *Black Dog?*" she mumbles, as they walk away from the animal patrol station.

The two of them stop for a moment and begin to laugh out a few dog barks. They see Nike flirting with Annie and Ruby. "It looks like a Golden Retriever convention," chuckles Bear. "And by the way-have you ever heard about the legend of Tuckernuck?" she mumbles to Katie.

Katie looks back at Bear with a surprising grin.

Bear and Katie say thanks to all the dogs who helped them and are now their friends: Little Bit the Dachshund and sweet little Cracker, Sophie, Tucker, Rascal, Muffy, and all the poodles, the Newfoundland, Sea Girl, the Rottweiler, Sybil. Stan the Chow/Lab Mix the

It's been quite an experience for the two of them. A tour of the Whaling Museum, something to eat, and a really long rest for the night is all a dog could want right now.

The End.

A LITTLE BIT ABOUT "LITTLE BIT"

A beautiful sweet and lovable Dachshund. She came to her owners when she was six months old. They shared nine wonderful years with her. Her name was appropriate for her small size. 'Little Bit' loved to play with small super balls because she could get three at a time in her mouth. She truly loved her best friend "Cracker." She and Cracker were always together. Together they enjoyed greeting people at the door, with a few sharp barks. But most of all, 'Little Bit' enjoyed sitting on her owners lap, watching television.

'Little Bit' was truly loved and will always be missed.

'JASPER THE CAT'

Our lovable cat Jasper. A solid gray cat with pretty yellow eyes. He appears in every Bear and Katie book. We called him our grey kitty and he was twelve years old. Jasper will surely be missed. And will continue to appear in the Bear and Katie series.

IN MEMORY OF

My very close friends Robert (Rob) and Angela (Angie) Bystrack, two very special people who will forever be missed. Their love for animals was noticed by everyone who knew them. Their two yellow Labs, Honey and Sugar are included in this story, especially for their daughter Cassie to enjoy.

ABOUT BEAR AND KATIE

Bear is gentle, caring, intelligent and quick thinking. She always obeys the rules and loves playing the part of Katie's protector. Her hobbies includes, riding around with Dad, retrieving balls and chasing squirrels. Bear welcomes a pat on the head from everybody she meets. Bear, a female BlackLab/Shepherd mix, wandered her way to our doorstep when she was only six weeks old. Bear always wears a red collar.

Katie is fun loving, a bit too friendly, and always getting into trouble. She loves her best friend Bear and knows she will always come to her rescue. Katie finds trouble everywhere she and Bear go. Her hobbies are swimming, retrieving balls and playing frizbee. Katie was rescued from a dog pound when she was six months old. Katie is a female Black Lab. She prefers to wear a blue scarf.

ABOUT THE AUTHOR

Loni R. Burchett was born in Ashland, Kentucky, and has lived in New Hampshire for sixteen years. Her love for New England always brings her back. *"I got my inspiration to write the Bear and Katie Series when I moved to New England. Everywhere I go I find something to write about."* She is a wife, mother of five and a devoted animal lover. Her hobbies are travel, art and photography. She lives in the Lakes Region of New Hampshire as well as her home state of Kentucky.

ABOUT THE ILLUSTRATOR

Michael Mayne is a native of Russell, Kentucky. Michael is currently rounding out a degree in *Visualist Design* aside from Illustrating. He enjoys creating narratives and characters of his own, while taking as many stories across as man mediums as he can. His appreciation for quality video games and movies-animation in particular-has set his sights on related career fields.

BEAR AND KATIE BOOKS IN CIRCULATION

The Great Searsport Caper
A Day at Nestlenook Farm
A Day with Friends
The Riverboat Ride

FUTURE BEAR AND KATIE BOOKS

Bear and Katie at the Kentucky Derby
(Run for the Roses)

Bear and Katie
Lost in the White Mountains

Bear and Katie
A Trip to the Big Apple
(New York-New York)

Bear and Katie
Meet Mr. Wanbli (Eagle)
and Mato the Bear

Bear and Katie go to Ireland
(Kiss of the Blarney Stone)